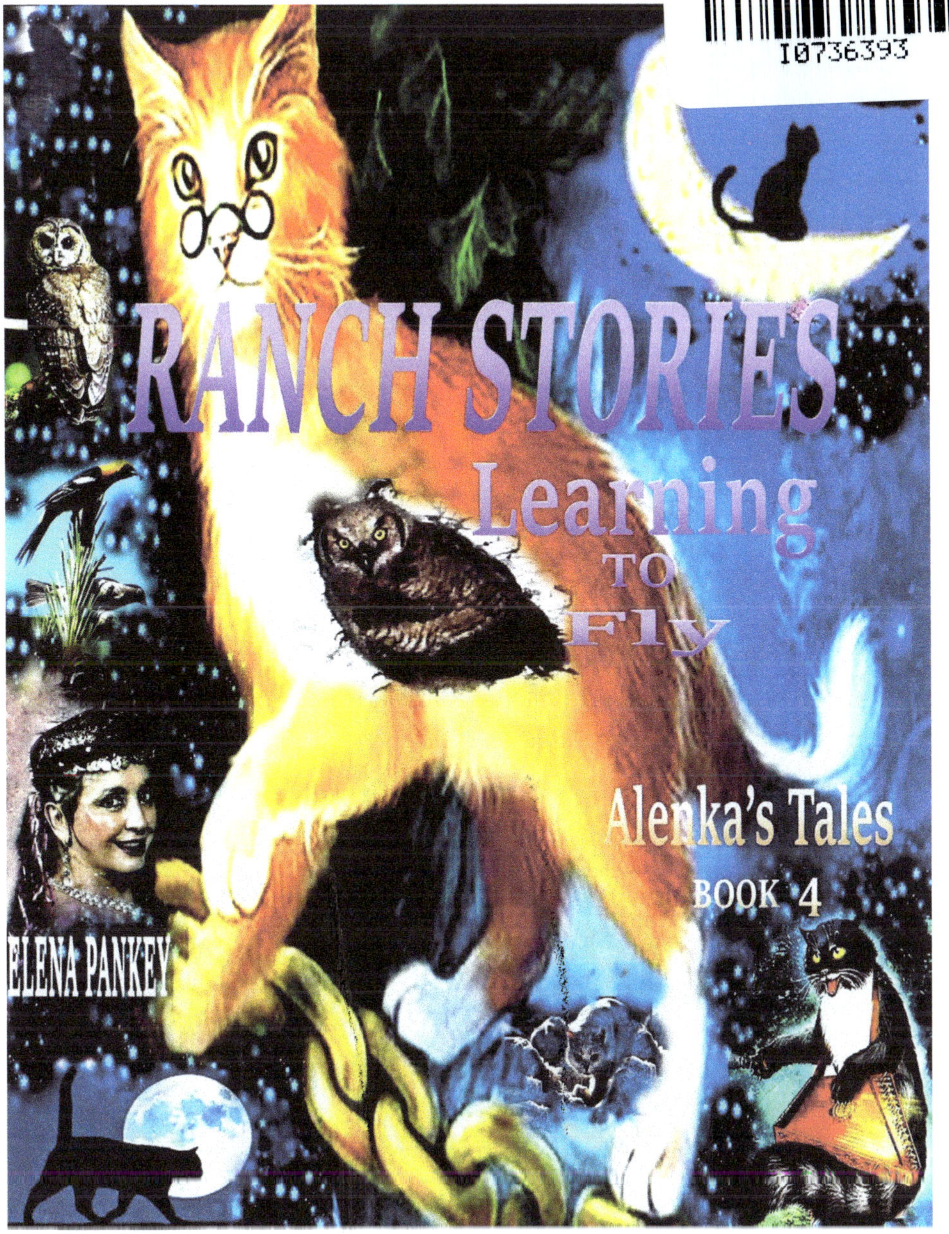

RANCH STORIES

Learning to Fly

Alenka's Tales

BOOK 4

ELENA PANKEY

978-1-952907-09-8

Learning to Fly
RANCH STORIES

***

Alenushka Tales
Book 4

Elena Pankey

***

ISBN: 978-1-952907-09-8

Contents

Introduction

The fourth book "Learning to Fly. Life at the Ranch," is the part of the Alenka's Tales series. The plot of the book is not developing on the Black Sea, as the first three books, but it is on the California Ranch.   Alenushka talks about her German shepherd dogs, who was protecting songbirds. It has an impressive story about a terrible meeting with the poisonous rattlesnakes, and how her dog barely survived after a fatal bite. It has an entertaining story about the rabbits who were sitting under the window, requiring a free supply of carrots. It has stories about small songbirds courageously fighting with the crows and protection their nests. It has an interesting story about the young Owl parents taught to fly their son and about their battle with the hawk; and others.

Alenushka thought: "*Well, this time we were lucky and saw the rattle snake in advance!* "

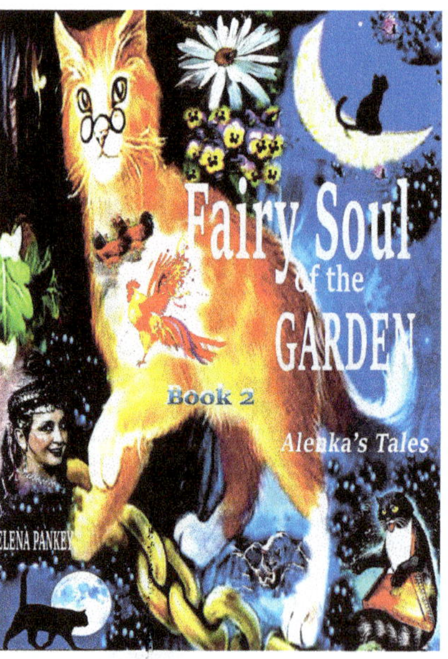

Garden Spirit

Ask and you will be given! I asked God for water, he gave me an ocean. I asked God for a flower, he gave me a garden. I asked God for a tree, he gave me a forest. I asked God for a friend, he gave me you. There is not enough darkness in the world to put out the light of one candle: The Candle of Love, Hope and Friendship. A candle loses nothing by lighting another candle".

***

It was a wonderful light and calm feeling in the garden where Alenushka grew up. It had absolutely unbelievable fragrance. Alenushka could stay there for hours hiding from all her troubles and came out of it feeling much better. At least she felt that the garden Spirit loved her, like nobody else.

Grandmother Anna was teaching Alenushka the basic law of gardening and life. *"You reap what you sow. Try to be kind, honest and compassionate. That's what you will harvest. Then, share the blessings and abundance of your garden, whether it is in the form of fruits, flowers, herbs or vegetables".*

The garden was providing food and shelter for wildlife. While sitting there in the bushes Alenushka trusted all around her. She watched the birds singing in the trees, enjoyed the lady bugs coming to her palm. She was curious about the always busy ants rushing back and forth. The girl loved all of them.

Especially she loved to stroll under the vine rows and pick up grapes. Usually there were small, black and very sweet grapes. Whatever she could find there in the garden was her main food source for the whole day. Also, the garden never knew any chemicals and had healthy plants. So, Alenushka could eat all things right there from the bushes.

Every spring her grandparents planted some potato and different vegetables. In June

they all went to the garden. Alenushka walked behind her grandfather who dug the pink, fresh potatoes, collecting them in the basket.

There was almost no rain in the summer. All plants were fighting for survival. The garden was refreshingly casual, connecting with the natural landscape. Irrigation had to be done by hand, carrying a little bucket with water.

The rabbits in the garden listened to Alenushka's songs, and even the honey bees stopped buzzing. Her dogs attentively were looking at their mistress with their clever brown eyes. The dogs were always ready to love, serve and comfort her.

Long ago Alenushka learned that many living creatures carefully and cheerfully lived in the same garden. Also, they taught her how to achieve all the most important things in the life, how to overcome all obstacles on the road to a dream.

The spirit of the garden gave her comfort and joy, and finally reflected in her personality. However, Alenushka only had her own garden thirty years later, when she moved to California.

***

Binding Threads

In the summer of 1991, after several years of absence, mother Emma returned to Gelendzik with her new husband. They were building a new house near the Black Sea, and planned to take Alenushka to live there. But Alenushka did not like her unpleasant, thin-lipped stepfather. Also, she did not want to leave her childhood place, where she was raised by her loving grandmother Anna. So, she tried to postpone that moment of separation. Alenushka was standing near the low window, looking into the garden and listening to the radio.

Suddenly the announcer indignantly broadcasted the shocking news. Twenty-year-old American student Victusha and his friend tried to hide a girl in the trunk of their car in order to transport her from East Berlin to West. But they were stopped, searched and sent to prison. The boy's grandmother, Emma, like all his relatives, was terribly worried, and tried to help him. Coincidentally, she had the same name as Alena's mother, which was a big surprise for the girl.

At that time, while listening to Soviet radio hysterically condemning the American students, Alena could not imagine that in some magical way, thirty-five years later, this boy Victusha would become her devoted and loving husband. Her mother came to her and took her hand: "*It is Time to go to live in our beautiful new house!*"

Then, Alena loudly and firmly declared: "*And I will live in America!*"

In the 1960s, during the outbreak of the Cold War with America, to wish such strange thing and in a loud voice was simply outrageous revolutionary blasphemy. So everyone just maliciously laughed at such an awkward, wild joke.

Invisible, connecting threads continued to weave the paths of fate and to connect the future with the present. The whirlwinds of fate, like the waves of a raging ocean, took off and fell, dragging a person along, and continuing to weave their invisible, connecting threads.

House on the Hill

Alenushka met the kind Knight Victusha in 1996, and moved to his citrus and avocado ranch in 1997. She settled with him in the big house on the top of the hill. In the 1950's his family owned about 3000 acres along the San Luis Rey River and along Highway 395.

The area around the Ranch house was surrounded by several dry, grey hills, and brown mountains. Since there were seldom rains in the area, the mountains and hills had dull, boring color all year around. The biggest, Lancaster Mountain, was very close to the house, and the inhabitants of the house had blocked horizon view on the East. For many years, the house on the hill was a very quiet, spacious and isolated place. Nothing was growing next to the house and nothing was in the front yard.

On the West side of Victusha's property there was a "bedroom district" with several rows of houses below the hill. Those rows of average houses were stretching to the Highway. That small town was built around a lake. But soon, that lake dried out, as well.

After rare and prolonged heavy rains the San Luis Rey River flooded out of its banks. That powerful, strong and wild water flooded both

sides of the river. After such rare and heavy rains, the inhabitants of the house were isolated in the living space, and saw only the thousands of orchard trees around them. But later the river dried out and many trees grew in its bottom.

The Ranch had its own wells, a very complex irrigation system, a cleaning system for drinking water and its own propane tank. Usually, the inhabitants of the house had a good supply of stored food for several locked-in days. When the dirt dried a little, Victusha got on his tractor and repaired the roads to the house and to the main gate to get out of the property.

Alenushka spent most of her time on the Ranch. Soon after moving in she began to plant cypress trees near the house, and made a special garden with fruit trees. One day her cat Tosha and the dog (an Alaskan Husky) were taken by the coyotes. Then

Alenushka asked Victusha to put a fence around the house hill, and got new dogs. The dogs were the best, smartest, courageous German shepherd. Alenushka was very happy with their devotion and love. They all were watching the changes which were going on around.

Slowly the area down below the hill got more houses, and the hum of the cars during the peak hours on the Highway reached the house on the hill. That noise of civilization increased significantly over time. That traffic noise of the passing cars hurrying from North to South was especially strong around 6 am when Alenushka walked her dogs.

Alenushka was born on the Black Sea; all her life she lived in a maritime climate. She was accustomed to enjoy seeing the sea every day. When she came to live in the dry, dusty ranch, she tried to drive to the ocean as often as possible. The ocean was forty minutes from the ranch, and one day Victusha got her a beach house. It was a wonderful resolution to all problems.

By the virtue of her energetic character and a vibrant personality, it was very difficult for Alenushka to live in such a quiet place. In Russia she was happy to have a very interesting and active life style, worked a lot, and moved all the time. Her grandmother

used to say that while we are moving we are alive. But the quiet life on the Ranch was a strong contrast to her exciting life in St. Petersburg, and a great challenge. Alenushka very slowly became accustomed to the quiet and isolation of the place where she was living.

But her every day communication was mostly with her dogs, who were very grateful and loving listeners. But the energetic and creative Alenushka mind was seeking a resolution. Later she found some consolation in teaching dances, organizing performances, and cruising around the world. Then she began to writer her ranch stories about everything that she observed there.

Finally, she planted a lot of different beautiful trees, bushes and flowers, creating her own gorgeous garden, which was heaven for her.

***

Night Music

Alenushka lived on the top of the hill, among the mountains, citrus and avocado trees. Some people were wondering if so isolated a ranch has any noise. Such surprising question told her that people don't listen to the nights.

If restful sleep would not come to Alenushka, then many different noises could bother her and keep awake. At the ranch the most pleasant time for Alenushka was in the winter.

Sometimes the wind or the rain outside made a very cozy sound, and then it was good to be safe and comfortable at home. Alenushka felt some rest or some relaxation when there was rain. The ranch had many different sounds. There were the grasshoppers, different insects, frogs and birds singing. Especially after the rain, through the open windows Alenushka could hear the loud chorus of frogs from the river. At about midnight, the coyotes were yapping, and the dogs replied back to them. Victusha's grandfather's old clock strikes each hour, loudly reminding of the passing life. But the new clock upstairs sang the music: "Life is going on".

When the irrigation system is working, the pump down below the hills in the orchard constantly makes assuring noise, reminding that everything is fine on the ranch.

Every night, Alenushka was listening to that night music, thinking about what to do next, and how to live. She felt that if she would just keep dancing, teaching, writing, traveling, or, better, cruising she could be happier. The ocean was cleaning her energy and helped her to live in the strange land among strangers.

Dogs

In the garden two German Sheppard lived. One dog was Tuzik and another one was Sonia. The yard had a special fence that the dogs would not run away to the orchard. The fenced yard around the house was huge, and it included a big hillside garden with different fruit trees, flowers and bushes. But the dogs were accustomed to do their private toilet business outside of it. Alenushka was happy about that habit of her dogs to keep her garden clean. Several times a day, she took her dogs for a walk on the different ranch roads.

Dog Sonia did not want to run around alone. She wanted to do everything together

with a friend. She was sure that her friend was Tuzik. But boy dog Tuzik was very jealous when the younger dog Sonia came to live on his property and she took all the attention of his owners. But since the owners loved her, Tuzik decided to be tolerant to her, as well. Later he became accustomed to the cheerful and playful Sonia.

She generally thought that her existence was to make everybody happy, wave her tail, and kiss everybody. That was her nature. Alenushka prohibited dogs to jump on her with the kisses and hugs. Then, Sonia learned that nice man Victusha did not tell her anything about it. So every time Sonia saw Victusha she jumped very high and kissed him. It was her way of saying; *I love you the most because you never scold us for anything.*

Since no strangers would come to the house, the dogs were bored without barking.

They wanted to do their job, to protect the house and property of the owners. But often there was nobody to protect from. From time to time, they were very happy when they could exercise their rights to work, and fulfill their duty to protect the property from all kind intruders. The happy time for the German shepherds was the time when the postman or delivery man would drive up to the house, or the pickers would come to get the avocados and oranges. Then, the dogs got excited, and barked with all their strength. After such well-done job they wanted to go out and to mark all the territory around. Then, they would

come back home with the desire to eat something delicious, even dry dog food was OK.

The dogs, Tuzik and Sonia, did not want to hunt neither rabbit nor squirrels. First, it was too hot during the day to hunt. Tuzik was already pretty old, and generally did not want move too much without a very good reason. During the hot day, they were too lazy to run around the garden. The dogs are waiting for Alenushka to go walking with them and tell them what they should do. So most of the day they just were lying down on the steps of their stairway or on the patio and did not want even to move their ears. But they enjoyed going to the swimming pool. This is why Alenushka bought for each of them their own pool. The dogs jumped in it on the hot days to cool off.

Also, from day one, Alenushka trained her dogs to go to the garage and exercise on the treadmill. Her garage was her dance studio. But she had two treadmill machines there. Dogs knew that they had to jump onto it and run for several minutes before getting their dinner.

Sometime, the young girl Sonia did not want to do such (useless as she was thinking) movement. So, when nobody saw her, she would jump off the machine and hide behind running Tuzik. So Alenushka started to tie her up to the machine, and Sonia learned not to do that without permission.

The dogs were very intelligent and knew many words. They were listening carefully to their owner, and watched her movements. They knew in advance what she wanted from them, and tried to do it to make her happy. But they enjoyed the exercise in the garage only on cool days and only because they wanted to please their owner.

***

Snakes

The area around the hills and the house is full of poisonous rattlesnakes. They start to move well when it is hot. Usually it is time from May and until almost until October. They are still there during the winter, as well. But they don't like the cold weather, and don't move much during the cool season.

Several times Alenushka saw the rattlesnakes when she walked her dogs along the ranch roads. When the dogs were very young they were taken to a special school, where they were taught to avoid the snakes. However, once at night, Tuzik did not see the snake in advance, and was bitten. He yelled from the terrible pain, but still while strongly limping came back home and told Alenushka to help him. His leg got swollen very fast. Right away Alenushka gave him two pills of vitamin K. She knew that vitamin K is good against the poison.

Then, she took her dog to the hospital, where the veterinarian doctor tried to save his life for the whole night. After that tragic event, Tuzik barely could handle the heat. The nerves in his leg were damaged, and he could not stop on hot ground.

Another time, during the evening before the sunset, around 6 pm, Alenushka walked with her dogs along the road near the persimmon trees. She always was holding her younger and highly emotional dog Sonia on the leash. But old Tuzik, as always, was freely running ahead of them. Suddenly, he stood silently and stretched his head towards the rattlesnake. The snake was about two meters in front of him. Alenushka and Sonia also stopped, stood still and waited.

They saw the terrible, poisonous rattlesnake was tightly folded into a tense coil, ready to attack. She apparently hunted for squirrels, and was ready to straighten her rings in a huge leap toward her victim. When the snake felt that Tuzik came too close to her, she began to rattle her tail with a terrifying sound that made everyone feel cold in the blood.

The snake hissed: *"I am your death! Do not come any closer!"*

Alenushka thought: *"Well, we were lucky this time! This snake at least warned us in advance!"*

And they went around her a long distance. But a minute later they heard from afar the terrible dying scream of a bitten squirrel. The snake got its dinner.

Another hot summer night a rattlesnake was chasing the mice and crept up to Tuzik's porch. It made a lot of menacing, threatening noise, ready to bite and kill anybody by her poison. Tuzik barked at her trying to get the snake away. But the snake felt it was trapped and raised her upper body ready to strike. Courageous Knight Victusha came out with a gun, shot the snake, and threw it from the hill. Fortunately, this time the evil plans of the snake did not work out for her. Alenushka washed the porch with chlorine.

She was thinking: *"To keep the family safe, to cherish the loved ones, everybody has to watch for the warning signs and be very careful."*

The ranch life continued to write its book. It just moved Alenushka's hand, putting everything that was happening around on the paper. The ranch was teaching: *"Do not trust even a smiling snake"*.

Rabbits

Alenushka office was in the low part of the house. While having a rest from writing, she looked out the windows. There were rabbits down there, trying to eat roses which grew under the window. It was the Mother rabbit. She smelled the beautiful fragrance of

the rose, and felt it was edible. Then, she stretched a little up to get to the flower. All around her was already just bare ground. She and her always growing family eat everything. Only green and beautiful bushes of the narcissus were still there. But their long green leaves and all parts were poisonous. Even though the rabbits were very hangry, they knew what was good for their health, and what was bad. The long, juicy leaves of the narcissus looked so green and delicious, but the rabbits could not eat them.

Periodically, Alenushka took photos of the Bunny family through the window of her office. Alenushka saw that next to the mother -Bunny her there children came out, to be on the sun and enjoy the beautiful day. One began to suntan on the rocks, periodically turning around and stretching his legs.

They lived under the Plumbego bushes, hiding from the dogs and from all other danger of the garden. When the fence was built around the house hill, they stayed in the garden, feeling happier because they felt more protected. Their father came for the weekend and in the evenings to visit his family. He lived outside of the fence, in the far end of the hill. But every day at dinnertime he always came to the garden to spend the evening with his family. They all usually had their dinner around the time of sunset.

Sometime, they all were sitting under the window and looking up. Clearly, they were saying: "*Alenushka! Go to the garden and bring us some delicious green grass. There is so much of it in the garden*".

Alenushka listened to them, saw their smart faces and went to pick the grass. One day she decided to buy a huge bag of carrots for them. She thought that bag would last for several months. Every day she threw several huge carrots to the garden. But in an hour all carrots were gone completely. Soon the huge bag, that she planned to have for the rabbits for a month, was also empty.

Rabbits happily looked up, saying: "*Thank you, God, for your generosity and for that rain of abundance! We hope your kindness would never end, and we would not need to work anymore for the food.*"

At the same time every day rabbits came out from their Plambego bush, where their house was. But still the rabbits did not go far from the bushes. They were afraid of everything, of any little noise around. They were sitting closer to the house while looking up at the window. Their eyes clearly were saying that they were hangry. Mother Rabbit loudly said that

Alenushka should better understand that they don't have any more carrots or grass around. And she should go and bring them some more food.

Alenushka wanted to make them happy. So, she went to the garden and brought more

green delicious grass to the rabbits. They were so delighted about the fresh, green food that suddenly fell from the sky. They were sitting, eating and praising God that he sent them such a feast.

Immediately a squirrel came out and began to chew something as well. Especially, squirrels loved the oranges that Alenushka often sent to them in the bushes. She lived under the same bushes, as well. They are all together - happy family. Happy Easter!

In June squirrels climbed to the apricot or almond trees, and ate all the fruits that still were on the branches. Alenushka learned that she needs to protect her fruit trees from the squirrels. So, she wrapped the tree trunks with metal sheets. This is how she kept the fruits for herself.

***

Ranch Birds

Many colorful birds live on the Ranch, especially around the swimming pool area and very close to the house, where it is safer. They are in the garden, as well, where there are so many constantly blooming flowers. The singing birds come in March, and right away they begin to look for partners with whom they could play their love games. March is a very noisy and busy time for the birds, especially very early in the mornings. They mostly are singing their beautiful songs of love and glorifying their joyful life. Alenushka put several birds' houses in the garden and they occupied them right away. It is pleasant to wake up to the birds' songs.

Then in April the birds finally formed their families and began making their nests.

The birds finally learned that their nests could be broken by crows and hawks. So they got smarter, trying to build their nests in more protected locations. They build their nests in the low part of the cypress and low parts of the palm trees, mostly inside the front yard.

In May the singing birds began to lay eggs in the nests and sit on them. Some already have small and loudly yelling babies. When Alenushka would be feeding her dogs, the baby birds also would be yelling very loudly because they are always hungry.

***

There were a lot of crows on the ranch. They busted songbird nests. The songbirds tried to settle closer to the house. But when no one was around, the snooty crows also flew close and ate the chicks. Alenushka jumped out of the house with a gun and shot at crows. But they never were hit. Although they were afraid even of her loud screams and waved hands. Dogs, learning from their mistress, and possibly out of the boredom and inactivity, became used to reacting to the crows, as well. They often looked up, saying: "*It is the time to do something drastically against these bold crows.*" The big shepherd, Tuzik, barked at the birds, urging the hostess to act immediately. Seeing Alenushka with a gun and dogs, the crows flew away so fast, that even their feathers rained down.

Loudly yelling in a nasty hoarse voice, the crows still were scared of people. But in their cowardly and insolent nature, it was customary to them to act out of the blue, out of cunning and meanness.

When the mother of a singing bird flew for food for her chicks, the crows were right there. They deceivingly flew to the unprotected nests and attacked the tender chicks. Once, a flock of crows flew up to the last palm tree on the western road and ravaged the nest of a falcon, who was out in the search of mice for his chicks. When the falcon came, she was in a big surprise to see her empty nest. She was just seating there, turning her head, and looked around whom to punish. But the crows already were far gone.

***

Tuzik periodically was expressing his concern about birds invading his property. Then he learned his new job in protecting the birds. He started to bark at the crows and hawks, warning Alenushka to come out with the gun.

Before, in the early morning, the crows came very closer to the house. They would be sitting on the palm trees, watching the birds. When Alenushka heard several bad, loud yelling of the crows, she would run out with the gun, and shoot towards them. The crows learned it. They stopped coming very close to the house to destroy the singing birds' nests. Other crows come silently at sunset, cruising around the palm trees and looking for the nests.

It is amazing that in the spring, when birds made their nests and fed their chicks, some birds were sitting high on the trees and looked out for the enemies. They were incredibly courageous, these little birds. And with all their bravery, they were guarding their nests.

Without hesitation, without fear, they ran at any size of enemy and rushed into the battle for protection of their offspring. Alenushka often saw a very small bird fearlessly pursuing a crow or hawk many times bigger than the singing bird. Sometimes, two little birds were chasing their enemies, actually, tried to peck them. But still they need people to help them.

In the spring very earlier in the morning, a lot of birds began to sing their greetings very close to the bedroom. Then, several bold crows would come and loud stamps on the roof of her bedroom. That crow was flying around, acutely yelling to the other crow to come to join her. Alenushka always jumped out of the house with the gun, which is always ready, standing in the corner. She was shooting towards the crow, trying to scare the big nasty birds away. This was how her days began.

***

Father's lessons

Different birds have different voices. Some sing loudly, and talk to each other actively throughout the day. Alenushka was watching one bird family who had a new son

Bobby. Every morning and before the sunset they come to get some food from the meadow in front of the door. Mother Bird immediately walks forward, far from her husband and her adorable, but a little noisy, son. She likes to enjoy her breakfast alone, in peace and solitude. Her husband is not as lucky as she, and cannot have one peaceful meal. Their son

is always hungry, and the father has to feed him.

Bobby is almost the same sizes as his parents, but he does not want to do anything for himself. He is running at his father's side, with wide open month, and with very loud cry: "Give me more - give more - give more!"

When he sees that his father got something from the under the grass, Bobby immediately pushed his open mouth to his father. The father does not have any choice, but to give him what he found. The baby bird Bobby tries to run as close as possible to his father, and yells almost without stopping. The squeaky, loud voice of the lazy son, his persistently open mouth, and his annoying begging for more food, is unbearable for his parents. Several different birds came, looked at this annoying scene, disapproved it, and escaped on their own business.

It looked like the hard working father did not have any time to eat for himself. He made strong effort teaching his son how to get food on his own. He had shown it to Bobby several times, and told him to try to do it independently. The baby bird picked randomly a couple of times without searching. He did not find anything, and gave up. He saw that it is much easier to acquire food from his father's work. Bobby continued run after his father with his widely opened mouth, loudly yelling: "more food, more food!"

Every day Alenushka could recognize the distinguished voice of the Baby Bird. But in several days, the father changed his techniques. When he saw some food down in the grass, he would stop near it, waiting when his son would come closer. Then, the smart father would run away from his hungry and unskilled son. But Bobby kept running after the father, demanding the food, instead of looking down and finding the seeds in the grass.

Once, his mother came close to them. She watched for a while, but soon she was annoyed by the yelling and the demanding voice of the baby bird. She quickly jumped between the baby and his father, and pushed the boy away. The baby bird was shocked by that action of his mother, stood for a moment with no yelling.

Since running away did not help, on the next day Father tried something new. He would find some good food in the grass and take it in his mouth. But instead of giving the food to his Baby Bird, his father was just holding the delicious snack in his own mouth, looking to a different direction. Several times the Father Bird would find the seeds, but he would keep it in his mouth.

His son first did not know what to do. Then, he looked around and looked down. He picked at the grass, but did not find anything. Then, he looked up, and opened his mouth. But his father did not give Bobby that desirable snack. Instead, he swallowed it himself! Moreover, that was not all. After that his father began to run away, yelling back: *"Try again, my son. All food is under your feet, just look for it!"*

Bobby did not have any other choice, but to pick up some food by himself. His father taught him a good lesson.

On the next morning after breakfast, Baby Bird and his parents had a family meeting. With joy and excitement, they stated, that their son had gained the skills of food finding. Now it was a different agenda, and his parents discussed it simultaneously with big excitement. It was time to teach him some social skills. Baby Bird said: "*Should I learn how to fit well in the Bird community?*"

The parents stopped talking for a while from this unexpectedly mature statement from their son.

Then Father said: "*God gave you parents. You will make friends by your own choice. When you will get them, keep them for a lifetime.*"

Mother said: "*We are happy only when we have someone to share our happy time with. The more you share the more joy you will feel, and the happier you will be.*" With these wise thoughts, they let Bobby alone.

On the next morning, the bird family was again on the meadow. Baby Bird was

respectfully walking between his proud parents, finding food on his own. When his effort was successful, he was very excited, but still tried to talk to his parents very politely. And they cheerfully, with attention, answered him.

It was obvious that Bobby had learned a very important

lesson. He learned that in order to succeed in the bird's society, it is very important to be pleasant to everybody around.

On the closest tree Alenushka saw one family of birds who were singing their glory to the new and beautiful day. She watched them for a while, and then went on her own human life.

***

Baby Owl

One evening it was the time to go out with the dogs before bedtime. Suddenly, the dogs got very excited, especially the big Tuzik. He tried to jump up and clime on the palm tree. Alenushka came closer and saw a very unusual animal, sitting upside down on the trunk of the palm tree. She called her kind Knight Victusha. He came out and said that it was a Baby Owl. It

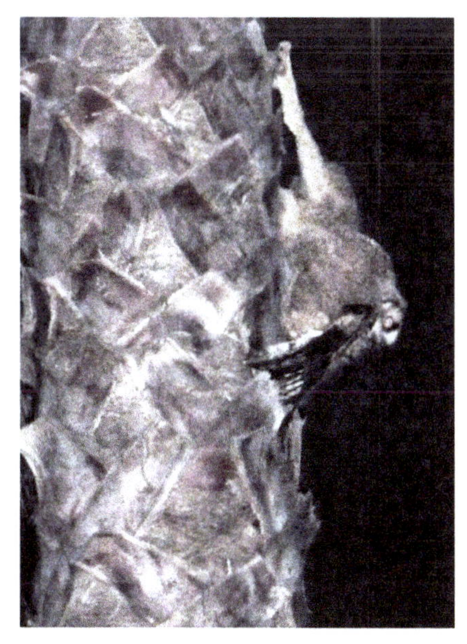

was his first night out from the mother's nest, and he did not know what to do with his wings. The Baby Owl stuck on the trunk of the Palm tree, and did not have any strength to move anymore. The voice of his mother was nearby, encouraging him to fly to her. The Baby Owl opened his mouth trying to tell her that he does not have any strength even to talk. But no sound came out of his mouth.

Alenushka had never seen such a small Baby Owl and wanted to help him. Therefore, she locked dogs in the front yard where they continued to have their excitement. Then, she went to the house and brought a long, soft and fluffy duster brush. Victusha handed the soft end of the stick with a brush on it towards the Baby Owl. The bird immediately grabbed it, and hanged upside down on it.

The Baby Owl was very cute and puffy. But he did not have strong wings and any

  knowledge about the world around. Victusha cared the bird to the bed of his truck. There, the Baby Owl lay down, feeling safe and resting. However, his mother was very upset that the people were interfering with her own business of teaching her baby how to fly. She was flying around, called her baby, still persuading her son to try to fly harder.

Alenushka went back to the yard to find some water and maybe just dog dry food to feed the bird. But when she came back, the bird was gone. So, the Baby Owl learned a little how to use his big wings. However, Alenushka was afraid that the bird might fell down close by and coyotes would get it. She asked Victusha to walk around with the strong flash light, looking for the Baby Owl. Soon, the owl was found. He was quietly sitting on the edge of the road, looking at the people with big innocent eyes. So, Alenushka went back home and brought the same long duster. The Baby Owl imminently grabbed it, hanged upside down, and they went back to the truck. Victusha said: *"Let's natures take its course..."*

But later at night, Alenushka still was worry about the bird and went to see what's happened. He was gone again from the truck. His mother's voice was far away. She still was teaching him how to fly.

***

That night they were happy to hear how the Owl father taught his cub to hoot as all Owls should to do. The father Owl was doing it first loudly and confidently. Then, he asked his baby to repeat it after him. But the cub just mumbled back something silly by his thin and tender voice. Their voices were clearly audible in the night. Nearby, a happy young mother Owl also taught something to the chick. Happiness and peace reigned in the night. How long such serene happiness would reign, how much time the happy family have on the ranch with no troubles from the wildness..

***

There were many tall palms trees along the western road. Victor planted them many years ago to protect his avocado trees from the strong setting sun. At the end of this road

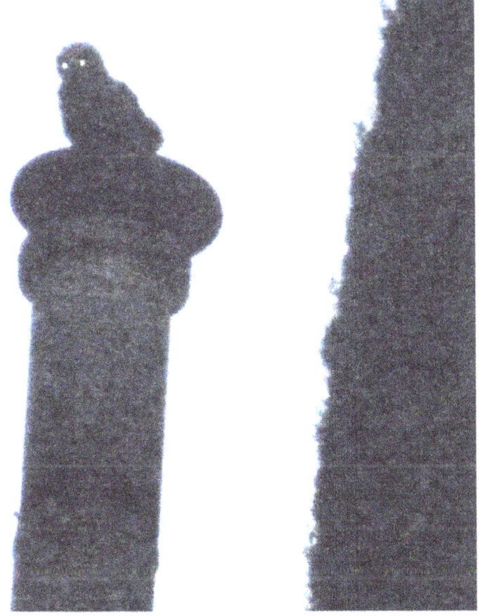

there was a hawk's nest high on the last tree. There were many of them breeding in the recent years on the comfortable ranch. Victor was happy of that, because they eat the rats, squirrels and other small animals. But Alenushka did not like these strong predators. Especially one of them bothered her all the time. He loudly and heavily shouted during the hunt, disturbing her soul. The hawks had more bold personality than the crows. Hawks flew very close to the house, ravaged the nests of songbirds, and eating the chicks. They were not afraid of either shots or screams.

***

The owl mother was sitting a little further from the baby, letting the father have the opportunity to express his love for their cub. Only occasionally she sent them her approval and her enthusiasm for the new successes of her son. His father taught him hunting lessons. The father-owl brought a mouse to the nestling, and the baby-owl was still enjoying a free breakfast in the parent's house.

The parents-owls were so much involved in the teaching their son that they did not notice that the night is over. The safe, comfortable dark night was their friend, but it was already gone. With the rising son, the danger of the daylight came for the owls. Alenushka and her dogs headed towards the house, reassured that the baby-owl continues to comprehend the basics of hard life at the ranch.

Suddenly, from the side of the last palm tree, where there was a hawk's nest, a terrifying, warlike cry started. Alenushka looked up. A huge hawk was rushing to the place where the father-owl was sitting with the chick. Alenushka tried to scare away that hawk, but he did not pay any attention to her waving hands and tiny yells. At the same time, but a little further, she heard a warning, excited cry of an owl-mother. But it was too late.

Owl-father tried to protect his little baby as courageously as he could, and covered his son by his body. But what could an owl do against a huge hawk.

The next night, walking before bedtime with dogs, no one heard the happy scream of an owl, the babbling of its new cubs, or the hoot of their father - owl. Over the ranch was an oppressive, deathly silence

Three days later, the owl mother began to search for her husband. She flew from one tree to another tree, visiting the places where they spent their happy time with her husband-owl. She called him very loudly, with desperation, in a dreary voice. Then, in the next night, she flew onto the roof of the house, where they on the moon light nights so often happily were meeting before. She screamed for a long time, with longing and despair. But no one responded to her call.

Alenushka could not sleep. She understood well the language of animals. And while for a long time living on a ranch, she learned to understand the language of birds. Finally she get up, walked outside, and said to the owl: *"If you find yourself a friend, fly in and settle closer to the house. And I will try to protect you from the hawks. "*

After this incident, Alenushka walked everywhere with her gun, trying to scare away the hacks and get a revenge for the gentle owls.

For the next three days, Mother Owl was silent. Then for several days she flew from tree to tree, sat next to the house, calling for her friend.

And suddenly, a Miracle happened, and her Friend flew to her. Life went on. Life was in a circle of eternity**...**

***

Did you know…

Owls are amazing birds. They form monogamous pairs, and settle only in pairs. Pairs of owls do not build their nests. They occupy crevices, hollows, or nests abandoned by other birds. Owls can breed one or several times a year, it all depends on the amount of food in the habitat. In a clutch there can be from 3 to 10 eggs. The female owl incubates eggs. A male owl is involved in feeding offspring. It is that different ages of birds live in the same nest. The parents feed all offspring, but priority is given to the oldest babies.

Owls are quite useful for the environment, because they destroy many harmful rodents. But owls never eat carrion. For the winter period, they make stocks and store them directly in the nest. The digestive system of this bird is designed so that they need to eat a whole carcass of the mouse.

In Egypt, owls were treated with respect and even mummified.

In the center of a Babylonian bas-relief was a woman with owl wings and paws. There were two owls depicted on the sides of her.

It is believed that this is one of the goddesses, and owls are her guards or companions.

In Christianity, the scream of an owl was considered a song of death. It symbolized desolation, loneliness, sorrow and solitude. For the ancient Slavonic cultures, the owl was reckoned as a demonic force. The bird was the keeper of underground treasures, and foreshadowed fire or death. In addition to the mystical symbol, the owl has always been a symbol of mind and wisdom.

God created the Garden of Eden with many beautiful trees and good fruits. There were the tree of life that can last eternal life, and the tree of knowledge of good and evil that brings death in the middle of the garden.(Genesis 2:16).

***

May the peace of my garden quiet my troubled hours.

May the beauty of my garden shine through my daily life.

May the inner strength of my garden give me courage.

May the dependability of my garden teach me faith.

May the joyous color of my garden fill my heart with song.

And may my garden vision unfold the wings of my soul.

***

Proverbs

We may travel far and wide, but wisdom and wit will always ring true. These sayings from countries all over this beautiful world reveal important lessons and universal truths for us all (Ariel Zeitlin).

***

"Truth is more valuable if it takes you a few years to find it." — French

***

"There is no shame in not knowing; the shame lies in not finding out." —Russian

***

"The pen is mightier than the sword." —English

***

"Fall seven times, stand up eight." —Japanese

***

"If you can't live longer, live deeper." —Italian

***

"Turn your face toward the sun and the shadows fall behind you." —Maori

***

"Some men go through a forest and see no firewood." —English

***

Author

The author – Elena Pankey - has created many fascinating books in Russian and English. Books are published in Europe and America. Among them, it is worth noting several funny books about the life of cats and dogs, about monuments to beloved animals. Her books about Argentine tango, about the famous Ukrainian artist Valeria Bulat, cannot be ignored.

Particular attention should be paid to her historical and biographical trilogy about Gelendzhik. It is extremely interesting to read about her memories of this city and its people who lived there 1950-1990.

The author has many years of experience in various fields of education, literature, theater, dance, cinematography. She especially enjoyed work as a guide in the Leningrad palaces and traveling with tourists in the Baltic States. She also shared with people her love of art and knowledge of the beautiful museums of St. Petersburg.

During the years of "perestroika", she had her own successful business, which gave her the opportunity to travel around the world. Finally, she found her true happiness in California. There she opened her dance school, was the producer of many shows and charity concerts. Many new books are also written there. Read: www.TangoCaminito.com

Rights Reserved

The title of the book is published in the United States of America. The first edition was in 2020. Photos, drawings created or redone by Elena Bulat. To obtain permission for any publication, write to the publisher at the address "Attention: Permission Coordinator" at: www.TangoCaminito.com